To Jean Rudnick,
Best Wishes,
fondly,

Dana

THE HICCUP CURE

Story and pictures by

Dara Goldman

G. P. Putnam's Sons   New York

Copyright © 1989 by Dara Goldman
All rights reserved
Published simultaneously in Canada
Printed in Hong Kong by South China Printing Company
Book design by Golda Laurens

Library of Congress Cataloging-in-Publication Data
Goldman, Dara. The hiccup cure.
Summary: After scaring Molly, Sam is apprehensive
when she says she has a cure for his hiccups.
[1. Hiccups—Fiction] I. Title.
PZ7.G5679Hi 1989 [E] 88-18428
ISBN 0-399-21663-4
First Impression

For my husband, Chuck, with all my love.
And for Alexander and Amy.

Sam liked to scare everybody.
In the morning he scared Muffin.

"Boo!" he shouted at his father.

"Boo!" he yelled at his mother.

At daycare, Sam hid behind a tree.

"Boo!" he shouted when Molly ran by. Molly jumped.

She didn't think it was funny.
But Sam did. He laughed so loud . . .

a hiccup burst out.

Then another . . .

and another . . .

until Sam's tummy began to ache.

"Drink some water," Miss Fay said.
"Hic," went Sam.

"Breathe into a paper bag," said Peter.
"Hic," went Sam.

"Put your head between your legs," said Amanda.
"Hiccup," said Sam.

"I know what *you* need!" said Molly.
"Look out," Peter shouted.
"Molly's going to pop the bag!"

"Molly!" said Miss Fay. "Don't do that."
"Just you wait!" Molly whispered to Sam.

All day, Sam wondered what Molly was going to do.
Something brushed by. Sam hiccuped.
But it was only Barney.

During lunch, Sam saw Molly crawl under the table.

Sam hiccuped.
But Molly was only getting her spoon.

At naptime there was a shadow on the wall.

But it was only baby Edgar's teddy.

Sam couldn't sleep. He was still hiccuping.
He looked for Molly, but she wasn't there.

Or there.

"Boo!" she yelled when Sam came near.

Sam jumped. He didn't think it was funny.
But Molly did. She laughed and laughed.

Suddenly a hiccup burst out of Molly.
But Sam noticed his hiccups had stopped.
Sam laughed!
"Now it's your turn, Molly!"